NINJA KID 9

NINJA FISH!

Scholastic Press
An imprint of Scholastic Australia Pty Limited (ABN 11 000 614 577)
PO Box 579 Gosford NSW 2250
www.scholastic.com.au

Part of the Scholastic Group
Sydney • Auckland • New York • Toronto • London • Mexico City
• New Delhi • Hong Kong • Buenos Aires • Puerto Rico

First published by Scholastic Australia in 2022.
Text copyright © Anh Do, 2022.
Illustrations by Anton Emdin and Jeremy Ley, 2022.
The moral rights of Anh Do have been asserted.
The moral rights of Anton Emdin and Jeremy Ley have been asserted.

ISBN 978 1 76112 048 0

 A catalogue record for this
book is available from the
National Library of Australia

Typeset in Bizzle-Chizzle, featuring Hola Bisou and Handblock.

Printed by McPherson's Printing Group, Maryborough, VIC.
Scholastic Australia's policy, in association with McPherson's Printing Group,
is to use papers that are renewable and made efficiently with wood from
responsibly managed sources, so as to minimise its environmental footprint.

 The paper in this book is FSC® certified.
FSC® promotes environmentally responsible,
socially beneficial and economically viable
management of the world's forests.

22 23 24 25 26 / 2

ANH DO

illustrated by Anton Emdin

NiNJA KiD 9

NiNJA FISH!

A Scholastic Press book
from Scholastic Australia

ONE

Hi! I'm Nelson Kane. Also known as

NiNJA KiD!

For the first nine years of my life, I was a pretty average kid. In fact, I might have even been a bit of a NERD.

Then something miraculous happened on my tenth birthday. I became

NiNJA KiD!

But I'm still a nerd . . .

SwOoSH!

My special ninja powers come from my dad, who **mysteriously** disappeared when I was young.

For years, no-one knew what happened to him. But I've finally worked it out. And it's all to do with **Dr Kane.**

You see, Andrew Kane is my dad's twin brother. When Dad and Andrew turned ten, my dad woke up with the skills of a ninja . . . but Andrew didn't.

This made him **furious.**

Luckily for him, my grandma is
an amazing inventor. To make up for
Andrew's lack of ninja skills, she taught
him everything she knew about inventing.

But Andrew stole Grandma's inventions
and became the **evil genius** known as
Dr Kane!

Dr Kane is constantly trying to make everyone flee our little town of Duck Creek.

He's unleashed **GIANT SPIDERS**, evil toys and even a **T-Rex!**

But Dr Kane doesn't work alone. He
has a chipmunk sidekick, Einstein, and an
assistant, known as the **ULTIMATE
NINJA.**

The Ultimate Ninja is actually my **DAD**. I think Dr Kane **kidnapped** him, and is controlling his mind with hypnotic powers. One day, I'm going to **free** my dad from the mind control and bring him home.

Home is a junkyard in Duck Creek. I live there with my mum, my grandma, our new dog, Noodles, and my cousin Kenny, who is always craving **FOOD!**

When I become Ninja Kid, Kenny becomes **H-DUDE**. He says the 'H' stands for **handsome!**

But sometimes I think it stands for **HUNGRY!**

Ninja Kid and H-Dude don't work alone either. We get **AWESOME** support from our friends Sarah and Tiffany.

Sarah and Tiffany don't know that Ninja Kid and H-Dude are actually me and Kenny!

H-Dude and I also get **ENORMOUS** help from Grandma and her `incredible inventions`. We think she's the **best inventor** who's ever lived!

Thomas Edison with the lightbulb!

Steve Jobs with the iphone!

Grandma is AWESOME!

Although, sometimes her inventions take a little while to work properly.

Like the **TOASTER KNIFE**, which is great when it works . . .

but **terrible** when it doesn't!

Or Grandma's **MegaGROW**
plant fertiliser, which makes veggies grow
extra fast. Only catch is, they never stop
growing!

Grandma has also invented the **Porta-house** – a house on legs! Only problem is, sometimes it **runs away** when you least expect it.

Grandma won't tell us about the **NEW**
invention she's working on.

She says it's a secret that she'll share
with us when she's 100% sure that it
works.

Kenny and I spent the whole afternoon guessing what the invention could be.

I guess we'll just have to wait to find out!

TWO

Kenny and I usually **LOVE** a carnival.

But just thinking about our upcoming **SWIMMING CARNIVAL** made us both feel a little sick.

Swimming doesn't come naturally to either of us. If humans were meant to swim, wouldn't we be born with flippers?

How can I describe our swimming style?
Hmmm. Have you ever seen a cat fall into
a bath?

MEooooOW!!!

That's how Kenny and I look when we're
in the pool!

But this year Kenny and I were determined not to come last. In fact, we had our hearts set on **winning!** And not just at our school swimming carnival. At the Regional Finals, too!

Sometimes, you have to dream **BIG!**

The reason we wanted to win so badly was because the prize was out of this world. The top four kids in the Regional Finals would win **FREE tickets** for their whole class to the Ocean Aquarium!

All aquariums are awesome. But the Ocean Aquarium is **extra** awesome. It's like the world's best SALTWATER ZOO!

They have the most colourful fish in the biggest tanks.

There are also penguins, seals and dolphins that can do tricks. And a brand-new star attraction . . .

THE
GIANT SQUID!

This thing is **HUGE!** It's as big as a minibus, with eight **loooooong,** scary arms. It's an

ENORMO-
SQUID!

GIANT SQUID

Kenny and I have been nagging Mum and Grandma to let us see the giant squid for weeks.

Mum said she'd love to take us but we can't afford it because the Ocean Aquarium is **super** expensive.

Charles Brock is the only kid from our school who's been to the aquarium. Charles is the son of the mayor of Duck Creek, and he's always **bragging** about the **amazing** things he's done. Charles has been everywhere!

If a kid ever gets to go to the moon, I
know who it will be . . .

Kenny and I are usually happy for our friends when they do cool stuff. But it's hard to be happy for Charles when he's such a **bully.**

Charles is also a really strong swimmer.
He cuts through the water like a **jet-**
propelled crocodile!

ZOOOOOM!

It was going to take **practice, practice** and more **practice** for us to knock Charles off his perch!

On the day before the carnival, Kenny and I went to our local swimming pool to train. Sarah and Tiffany were there, too.

I don't know why Sarah and Tiffany thought they needed practice – they can both swim like **dolphins!**

We also saw Billy Bob and Charles at the pool. Billy Bob wasn't a great swimmer, but his **mullet** acted like a winged keel, giving him extra **SPEED.**

Even when he was just practising, Charles was a **BAD sport.** He splashed water into the mouths of other swimmers as they were about to take a breath.

Take that, loser!

SPLASH!

Kenny and I stayed well away from Charles. We didn't want him stopping us from reaching our goal of **ten laps each.** But even without Charles splashing us, we still **struggled** to complete one lap!

While our techniques were OK, Kenny and I were **terrible** at taking a breath when we swam. Both of us needed to come up for air after **every** stroke, totally slowing us down.

GULP!

When Kenny and I **finally** finished our one and only lap, we climbed out of the water, **tired** and **disappointed.**

There was **no way** we were going to make it to the Regional Finals. To cheer us up, Kenny bought a bag of mixed lollies. A **MEGA bag** of mixed lollies!

When we arrived home, Grandma called out to us, 'Boys. Over here! Quickly.'

Grandma had a **huge smile** on her face, which could only mean one thing . . . she'd finished her new invention!

'What is it, Grandma?' I asked curiously as we stepped inside her workshop.

'Please tell me it's food related,' Kenny said. **I'm starving!**

Kenny was always starving.

'My new invention won't fill your stomach,' Grandma said, 'but it **WILL** fill you full of confidence!'

'You mean you're going to make me **even better looking?**' said Kenny with a grin.

'Not quite, Kenny. You're fine just the way you are,' she replied.

'Come on, so what is it, Grandma?' I asked.

'I know you two are desperate to do well in the swimming carnival,' Grandma said.

'We want to **win!**' Kenny said.

'Only problem is,' I said, 'we have to stop swimming every time we take a breath.'

'That's why I've created a **necklace** that allows you to breathe underwater!' Grandma said.

AWESOME!

'That is a **totally brilliant** idea!' I said.

'Can we try them out now?' Kenny asked.

'Of course,' Grandma replied, leading us out of her workshop. 'Jump into your bathers and you can have a swim in our **HUGE swimming pool.**'

'Ah . . .' I stammered. 'We don't have a huge swimming pool. We don't have a swimming pool **AT ALL!**'

'We do now!' Grandma replied.

She dialled her size converter up to **MUCH, MUCH BiGGeR** and aimed it at an old sardine can in the junkyard, which was full of rainwater.

ZAP! Within seconds, the can expanded to the size of a **HUGE** swimming pool.

'That is ridiculously **AMAZING**, Grandma,' I said.

'Wait until you try the necklaces!' she replied excitedly, handing one each to me and Kenny.

Kenny and I put on the necklaces, jumped into the pool, and started swimming. Not needing to come up for a breath meant we swam **HEAPS** faster than usual.

ZOOM!

I could have swum for days. It was amazing!

This time when we climbed out of the pool, we were dripping with **excitement!**

'This is exactly what we need for the swim trials!' I said.

'Just call me **SUPER-FISH!'** said Kenny. 'This is the best invention ever! Thank you, Grandma!'

'Happy to help my two favourite boys,' Grandma said proudly.

That night, Kenny shovelled down **THREE** portions of lasagne. 'Don't worry, everyone, I'm in training. It's called **carb-loading!** he said.

But I couldn't stop thinking about the necklaces and the swimming carnival. Maybe Kenny and I would qualify for the Regional Finals after all!

THREE

Next morning, I woke up feeling VERY strange. I'd never been confident before a swimming carnival before! Well, except for the year Kenny and I were in charge of the **cheer squad** and didn't have to swim.

'**Extra,** **extra,** read all about it! Blue's gonna **WIN** and there's **NO DOUBT ABOUT IT!**'

'Shout it to the **EAST!** Shout it to the **WEST!** When we hit the water, Blue team's **THE BEST!**'

'Coming down the waterslide landing on a **CACTUS,** **ALL** the other teams need more **PRACTICE!**'

The first race of the day was the Boys **25-metres** freestyle. Kenny and I took a deep breath then stepped up to the blocks.

'You've got this, Kenny,' I said.

'We've **both** got this!' he replied.

But it wasn't all good vibes.

'Should you two really be here?'
Charles heckled. 'I think the **kiddie pool**
is more your size!'

Charles' friends snickered at his lame
put-down.

'You're about to **eat your words,**
Charles,' I replied.

'Or drink them!' Kenny added.

The official started the race and
everyone dived into the water gracefully.
Except me and Kenny . . . we did

BELLY FLOPS!

SPLAT!

It was a **terrible** start. But, thanks to the necklaces, it didn't take us long to catch up to the others.

Usually when I'm in a swimming race, I can see all the other kids **waaaaaay out** in front of me. But this time, all I could see was the finish line. In the last ten metres, Kenny and I went stroke for stroke.

We finished **equal first!**

The next race was the Girls 25-metres freestyle. Tiffany and Sarah **blitzed** the field and finished first and second.

Sarah and Tiffany also won the backstroke, breaststroke and butterfly. So did Kenny and I!

Sarah and Tiffany tried not to look **surprised** at how much we had improved.

At the end of the carnival, Mr Fletcher announced that the four of us would be representing the school in the **Regional Finals.** Kenny and I couldn't have been more excited!

In the week before the Regional Finals, Tiffany and Sarah swam every day at the local pool after school.

Kenny and I wanted to practise, but other things got in the way. Like **ice-cream!**

Anyway, surely with Grandma's necklace, we were bound to win . . . **right?!**

On the day of the Regional Finals,
Mr Fletcher and the rest of our class took
the morning off school to come and cheer
us on! Billy Bob was leading the cheer
squad.

Once again, the day started with the Boys 25-metres freestyle. The kids in the other lanes were **HUGE!**

Kenny and I were in lanes three and four. As we stepped onto the blocks, Billy Bob and our **cheer squad** cheered so **LOUDLY** the grandstand was shaking!

'Pork chops, pork chops! Greasy, greasy! Nelson and Kenny will win this EASY!'

The race was about to start when an announcement came over the loudspeakers.

'Could the swimmers in lanes three and four please remove their necklaces.

'Ah, which lanes are we in?' Kenny asked.

'Three and four!' I replied.

'No jewellery is permitted in the Regional finals,' the announcement continued. 'Repeat, *NO jewellery.*'

Kenny and I exchanged **horrified** looks as we took off our necklaces and put them with our clothes.

As we returned to the blocks, I turned to Kenny. 'You know what?' I said. 'This is probably a lot fairer.'

'You're right,' Kenny said. 'But right about now I'm regretting eating all that **ice-cream** when we should have been practising!'

'On your marks,' the official bellowed.
'Get set . . .'

Kenny and I shared a nervous look.
BANG! The official fired the starting
pistol and the other swimmers executed
perfect dives.

Kenny and I did our standard
belly flops.

We were red and sore, and without the necklaces, we had to come up for a **breath** after each stroke. We eventually made it to the end of the pool.

But by then the medal presentation was **over!**

The same thing happened in the backstroke, breaststroke and butterfly finals.

Kenny and I came **last** and **second last** every time. At least we were consistent!

We weren't the only ones **disappointed** by our results. Sarah and Tiffany narrowly lost all their races to the Salmon twins from Duck Heights.

The four of us had arrived at the finals hopeful of **winning** Ocean Aquarium tickets for all our friends. We left with our tails between our legs.

FOUR

On the bus ride home, Kenny, Sarah, Tiffany and I felt as **flat** as pancakes.

But we refused to give up on our Ocean Aquarium dream.

'I want to see that **giant squid** so badly,' Kenny said.

'There must be another way we can get our class to the aquarium,' I said.

'But how?' Tiffany asked. 'It would cost **hundreds of dollars** if we all had to pay for tickets.'

'Sounds like we need a **BIG BRAINSTORM!**' Sarah said excitedly.

'Welcome, everyone,' Sarah announced from her bus seat, 'to our first official **Ocean Aquarium Brainstorming Session.**'

She was really into this!

'The first rule of brainstorming,' Sarah said, 'is that there is no such thing as a bad idea.'

'I **love** that rule!' Kenny said. 'My first idea is that we build our **own** aquarium and get our **own** giant squid.'

'Thanks for that idea, Kenny,' Sarah said, diplomatically. 'Does anyone have an idea that's a little more . . . **realistic?**'

'We've got a **new pool** in the junkyard,' I said. 'What about we invite the giant squid over for a swim?'

'I don't think the squid is allowed out to visit people!' Sarah said. 'Surely you've

got a sensible suggestion, Tiffany?'

'I **totally** do,' Tiffany said. 'There's
a promotion at the supermarket where
if you spend $200, you get a half-price
aquarium voucher. So we just have to
rustle up $200 each!'

'I like your thinking, Tiffany,' said
Sarah, 'but that's **way more expensive**
than paying for aquarium tickets in the
first place!'

'I've got another idea,' Sarah said. 'What about we get all the kids in our class to bring their **pets to school.** And then we put on a pet show!'

'I know you said there's no such thing as a bad idea,' Kenny said. 'But how does a **pet show** help us get everyone to the Ocean Aquarium? Does someone in our class have a **giant squid** for a pet?'

'No, they don't. But we'll charge our teachers and parents a couple of dollars each to watch the show,' Sarah replied.

'That'll bring in enough money for everyone in our class to buy an aquarium ticket.'

'That's **genius!** I said.

'Thanks, Nelson,' Sarah said. 'I knew you'd be on my wavelength.'

'Who's in favour of the pet show?' I asked the group.

All our hands shot up!

'Excellent!' I said. 'We're putting on a pet show to raise money for an Ocean Aquarium excursion!'

FiVE

In preparation for the pet show, we spent loads of time with our pets, trying to work out routines.

Sarah tried to teach her pug, Puggy, a few basic tricks. Only problem was, Puggy couldn't even remember his own name.

Puggy, sit!

Tiffany tried to teach her cat, Furball, not to **SWIPE** at everyone walking past.

Charles taught his pony, Fancypants, to do an entire *fancy* routine.

Poor Billy Bob couldn't teach his llama, Wally, anything because Wally kept **spitting** at him!

Kenny and I spent every second we could with our **awesome** new dog, Noodles. We had a huge advantage, thanks to Grandma's incredible **animal translation helmet.**

The helmet helps you speak to any animal in its own language.

Using Grandma's helmet, Kenny and I could **speak** **doggie** to Noodles. This meant we could teach her things other pet owners could only dream of.

Sarah, Tiffany, Kenny and I spent hours preparing the school assembly area for the pet show. We set up a stage and a section for the audience. And we decorated everything with pet-themed posters and streamers.

By the time we'd finished setting up, we were exhausted. But it was all worth it – tickets for the show **SOLD OUT** in minutes!

Kenny and I were the **HOSTS** of the pet show.

We **dressed to impress,** wearing top hats and velvet jackets. We also hired fancy microphones!

Sarah and Tiffany were in charge of presenting the awards, and were dressed to impress, too! They were *stylish, elegant,* and looked **totally awesome.**

They handed out voting forms to the audience and everyone was asked to vote **1, 2** and **3** in several categories.

The animals were a **hit** from the very first **SQUAWK!**

The capital of Eritrea is Asmara.

93

Even when the animals **didn't** do what their owners wanted them to, they were still **super entertaining.**

Like Puggy, who managed to do the **exact opposite** of what Sarah said. **EVERY SINGLE TIME.**

Puggy, roll over!

Puggy, shake!

Puggy, beg!

Tiffany introduced Furball as her
INCREDIBLE NON-SWIPING CAT.
But Furball tried to swipe Tiffany and
everyone in the front row as soon as he
stalked onto the stage.

The crowd thought it was hilarious!

Next to perform was Noodles. Kenny and I taught Noodles to run up a steep ramp, **leap** onto a floating platform, hit a lever to release a wreath of flowers, then **JUMP** through the wreath so she was wearing a necklace of fresh blooms.

The crowd went **absolutely WILD.**

Sarah and Tiffany read out most of the awards, and then it was time for the **finale.**

'Well now,' Sarah said, 'the time has come for our major award . . .'

'**Best in show!**' Tiffany announced excitedly.

Everyone was on the edge of their seats. Even the pets!

'And the winner is . . .' Sarah announced dramatically, as Tiffany opened the final envelope of the night.

'**Noodles the Moodle!**' Tiffany said excitedly.

The crowd went **nuts**. Kenny and I went **nuts**. Noodles went **nuts!**

WOOHOOO!

It felt **AWESOME** to win best in show. But it felt even more awesome to raise **enough money** for the whole class to go to the aquarium.

We did it!

SiX

The morning of our aquarium excursion, Kenny and I shovelled down breakfast.

'**Slow down!**' Mum said. 'You'll make yourselves sick.'

'Sorry, Mum,' I said. 'We're just super excited about seeing the giant squid!'

'Yeah,' Kenny said. 'I'm going to give it a **high eight!**'

Kenny and I excitedly packed our bags for the excursion.

'We should take our bathers and the underwater breathing necklaces,' Kenny said.

'Why?' I asked. 'There's no swimming pool at the aquarium.'

'I heard they sometimes choose a few kids to **swim** with the squid,' Kenny said. 'And if we wear the necklaces, we'll be able to stay underwater with it for ages.'

'That would BE AWESOME!' I replied.

'Maybe we should take Grandma's animal translation helmet, too,' I said.

'Totally!' Kenny replied. 'How cool would it be to **talk** to a giant squid!'

'That would be the **best thing ever!**' I replied.

What's it like being a giant squid?

I love it! Even sharks don't mess with this guy!

'Do you know what else we should bring?' Kenny asked.

'What?' I enquired.

'Noodles!' Kenny replied. 'She won best in show. She deserves to come.'

'Are dogs allowed in aquariums?' I asked.

'Dogs are allowed everywhere these days,' Kenny said. 'I can carry her in my **backpack!'**

Kenny was right. Noodles was very welcome at the aquarium. In fact, she was even more **popular** than some of the sea creatures!

The aquarium totally lived up to our expectations. The penguins were so cool. Literally! They did **belly-slides.** They **clapped.** And they danced – *ballet* . . . HIP-HOP . . . even BALLROOM DANCING!

The **seals** were also in top form. They were jumping and waving to us!

Then two of them dived in sync off ridiculously HIGH diving boards.

The dolphins had a bag of tricks.

Front flips.

Back flips.

One of them even did a card trick!

Suddenly, loud music **BLASTED** through the speakers. Then came the announcement we'd all been waiting for. 'It's time for the **giant squid show!**'

Everyone raced to the big pool in the middle of the aquarium. Kenny, Sarah, Tiffany and I managed to get seats in the **front row!**

An excited **ANIMAL TRAINER** ran out wearing a shiny black wetsuit and holding a waterproof microphone.

'She has the **coolest job** ever,' Sarah whispered.

'And the **wettest!**' I replied.

'Are you ready for the Ocean Aquarium's **BIGGEST** star?' the animal trainer asked.

We all cheered, clapped and shook our arms like they were squid tentacles!

'Please don't be intimidated by her size,' the trainer said. 'Because squids are harmless.'

'They're definitely not **armless**,' Kenny said. 'They have **eight** of those!'

'They also have two tentacles,' Tiffany said.

'And the tentacles are even **longer** than the arms,' Sarah added.

They were even more into giant squids than me and Kenny!

More loud music **BLASTED** from the speakers.

'It's almost **Squid O'Clock**,' the animal trainer announced. 'Please count down with me . . . **10, 9, 8 . . .**'

We all stood up and counted too. '**7, 6, 5, 4, 3, 2, 1 . . .**'

'Here she is,' the animal trainer said.

'**THE ONE,**

THE ONLY,

GIANT SQUID!'

The giant squid swam through a glass tunnel and into the pool. Then she popped her head above the surface of the water.

Her giant eyes stared at us. Then she winked! The crowd went

BERSERK!

'Most of you probably know that squids are **highly intelligent,**' the animal trainer said.

Sarah and Tiffany nodded to each other knowingly.

'Now let me **prove it!**' the trainer said.

We watched, amazed, as the giant squid completed a complex obstacle course. She SQUEEZED into a tunnel, **DARTED** through an underwater maze, then **swam** underneath a giant arch.

We were in total awe of the giant squid's intelligence. It was the **BEST** day ever until . . . the squid began acting **VERY** strangely.

First, she pushed the animal trainer into the pool when she wasn't expecting it. Then she splashed some well-dressed people in the back row who did **NOT** want to get wet. She was behaving like Charles Brock!

SPLASH!

'Seems our girl is a little **mischievous** today,' the trainer said as she climbed out of the pool.

The trainer had only just finished her sentence when the squid suddenly pulled her back into the water.

'Do you think this is part of the show?' Sarah asked.

'I don't think so,' I replied as the giant squid **hurled** the trainer into the crowd. Luckily, she was caught by a bunch of musclebound tourists.

'The giant squid's either having a bad day,' I said, 'or she's not what she seems.'

Suddenly, we heard a loud noise from above . . .

WUP! WUP! WUP!

A **helicopter** appeared above the aquarium. I recognised it instantly.

'That's Dr Kane's helicopter,' I whispered to Kenny.

'Are you sure?' Kenny replied.

Dr Kane stuck his grinning head out of the helicopter window.

'Yup!' I said.

The squid leapt into the crowd and tried to grab eight kids at once. She was so fast and agile – like a **SQUiD NiNJA!**
    The kids **screamed** and **squirmed** and narrowly avoided being pulled into the pool.

AAAAARGH!!!

As the squid **dragged** herself back into the water, one of her legs scraped against a seat and ripped a chunk of skin off. Underneath the skin was a **metal leg!**

'That's not a giant squid,' Sarah said. 'It's a **GIANT ROBOT!"**

Sarah was right. The giant squid was robotic. But how was Dr Kane controlling it?

'I can't see his chipmunk sidekick,' Kenny said.

'Or the **ULTIMATE NINJA,'** I added.

'Maybe Dr Kane's doing his own **dirty work** for once,' Kenny said.

Dr Kane was loving the **shock** on everyone's faces when they realised the squid was a robot.

Four security guards ran towards the squid to try and stop it. But the squid quickly **wrapped them up** with its long legs and threw them into the pool.

FLING!

The other animals were **terrified** by the giant robot squid's antics. The penguins were so frightened, they stopped dancing and hid in their igloo.

The seals put their **flippers** over their eyes, hoping the squid couldn't see them.

As the turtles tried to escape the giant squid, one of the babies got separated from its parents.

There was **TOTAL** *chaos* as everyone rushed to escape the aquarium.

Charles **pushed** all the other kids out of the way so he could escape first.

Get outta my way!!!

SEVEN

'I think it's time for Ninja Kid and H-Dude to make an appearance,' I whispered to Kenny.

'100% agree!' Kenny whispered back.

I stood up and turned to the others. 'I'm just going to the bathroom,' I announced.

'Oh, great idea,' Kenny added awkwardly. 'Me too!'

'**Now?!**' Tiffany asked, surprised.

'There's a giant robot squid tearing the place apart,' Sarah added.

'When you've gotta go, **you've gotta go!**' Kenny replied.

We quickly made our way through the panicked crowd to avoid further questions.

Fortunately, the bathroom was empty.
Kenny and I jumped into a cubicle each
and quickly changed into our Ninja Kid
and H-Dude outfits. We also put on
Grandma's **underwater necklaces** for
good measure.

And grabbed the animal translation
helmets for **extra good measure!**

H-Dude and I raced back to the pool deck.

'Everyone **stay calm**,' I announced, using the waterproof microphone. 'H-Dude and Ninja Kid are here to protect you.'

I mustn't have sounded very convincing because people continued running to the exits, **screaming!**

'Let's hope we have **more luck** calming the locals,' Kenny said, as the giant squid chased a seal around the pool.

'I'll **distract** the squid,' I said. 'You look after the other animals.'

'Dealio!' Kenny replied. Then he jumped into the pool.

And did another

BELLY FLOP!

'Hey, Dr Kane!' I shouted up to him. 'If your giant squid wants a new playmate, I'm available!'

'Oh, it will **love** that,' Dr Kane said, smirking. 'You've **bitten off** more than you can chew this time, Ninja Kid.'

As the giant squid stopped chasing the seal and slowly made its way towards me, I started thinking Dr Kane **might be right!**

H-Dude swam towards the baby turtle,
which looked sad and scared as it hid
behind a rock.

'I'm H-Dude,' Kenny said, using the
animal translation helmet. 'What's your
name, little guy?'

'My name's **Toot!**' the baby turtle
whimpered.

'Don't worry, Toot,' Kenny said. 'I'm
going to help you find your parents.'

Toot was relieved to have H-Dude's
help. And shocked he could **speak turtle!**

A dolphin swam past and Kenny used the helmet again. 'Excuse me, Ms Dolphin,' he said. 'Could you please help me find Toot's parents?'

'Of course,' the dolphin replied. 'Hop on!'

Meanwhile, the giant squid tried to sandwich me between its two long tentacles.

I leapt as **high** as I could and did a **spinning kick.** It was just enough to fend off the tentacles.

The giant squid surged towards me again. This time, it hurled all eight legs at me at once.

I raced along the edge of the pool and used my momentum to **jump over** the legs as if they were hurdles!

LEAP!

I knew I wouldn't be able to run from the squid forever. I had to think of something **FAST!**

Kenny was still riding the dolphin around the pool, looking for Toot's parents. They passed a seal and Kenny asked, 'Excuse me, Mr Seal. Have you seen Toot's parents?'

'Sure have,' the seal said. 'They're just round that bend.'

As **H-Dude** rode the **dolphin towards** **the bend**, he couldn't resist winking at Tiffany in the crowd.

Kenny was relieved to find Toot's parents hiding in a cave. But not as relieved as Toot and his mum and dad. They wrapped him in a warm turtle hug.

'We were **So worried** about you,' Mama Turtle said.

'Thank you for helping our son,' Dadda Turtle said to H-Dude.

'My pleasure,' Kenny said. 'He's been extremely brave. He's really starting to **come out of his shell!** I'd love to stay for more turtle chats, but I'd better help my friend fight the giant squid!'

EiGHT

H-DUDE joined me just in time. The giant squid had pulled me into the pool and was about to squeeze the life out of me.

'Hey, Squiddy!' Kenny said, looking the giant squid in its ENORMOUS eyes. 'Leave my friend alone before I TURN YOU INTO CALAMARI!'

'You're even more stupid than your stupid friend,' Dr Kane shouted to H-Dude.

'Oh yeah? Well you're–'

Before he could finish, the giant squid
wrapped its tentacles around Kenny then
threw us both high into the air.

Kenny and I **SPLASHED** into
the water and sunk to the bottom of
the pool. It was lucky we were wearing
our special necklaces because we were
underwater for **AGES.**

The second we burst through the surface of the pool, the squid grabbed us again. This time it **banged** our heads together. Luckily we were still wearing our helmets or our heads would have **cracked like coconuts!**

OUCH!!!!!

Dr Kane **laughed** so hard he almost fell out of his helicopter. Then we heard someone else laughing.

A high-pitched cackle was coming from **inside** the giant squid's head.

It was Einstein! Dr Kane's chipmunk sidekick was controlling the giant squid!

Kenny and I held a quick strategy meeting in the pool. 'If we can force the chipmunk out of the control booth,' I whispered, 'maybe that will cause the giant squid to **shut down.**'

'Good plan,' Kenny said as we swam to the side of the pool. 'Quick question. How do we force the chipmunk out of the control booth?'

'If we can get the squid to turn **upside down,**' I said, 'Einstein will fall out.'

'Great idea,' Kenny said. 'Another quick question. How do we get the squid to **turn upside down?!**'

'Follow me!'

We **raced** around the pool and
stopped underneath the tall diving
boards that the seals jumped off earlier.

'One each!' I said.

'Oh no . . .' Kenny groaned.

'**Oh yeah!**' I replied, racing up the
ladder.

Kenny remained frozen at the **bottom** of his diving **board**. The giant **squid** scurried towards him.

'You've got this, H-Dude!' I called down from my diving board. 'You've been on **rollercoasters** heaps higher!'

'I guess so,' Kenny replied, tackling the first few rungs.

But rollercoasters have seatbelts!

The giant squid threw its huge tentacles towards Kenny, but he made it onto the diving board just in time to narrowly avoid them.

The diving boards were **So HIGH** that the giant squid couldn't reach us with either its arms or its extra-long tentacles.

'C'mon, Squiddy,' I said. 'We want to keep playing.'

'Are you **crazy?**' Kenny said. 'This is a terrible playdate!'

'Trust me!' I said.

'Fine,' Kenny said. 'But if we get out of this, you owe me a block of chocolate – **FAMILY SIZE!**' Then he called down to Einstein. 'Let's play tag, Squiddy.

You're IT!'

'**What are you waiting for?!**'
Dr Kane bellowed at Einstein. 'Get them!'

'I **really** hope you know what you're doing, Ninja Kid,' Kenny whispered to me from his diving board.

The giant squid lurched out of the water. It was clearly a struggle for the massive metal creature to leap but it managed to **hurl** its two extra-long tentacles towards us.

Kenny and I were about to be ensnared again when I shouted, 'H-Dude, jump!'

'What?!' Kenny replied in disbelief.

'JUMP!' I repeated.

We both jumped as high as we could off the diving boards.

AAARGH!

The giant squid was forced to climb
even higher out of the water to try
and catch us. It was too much for its
enormous robotic frame and it flipped
upside down.

Einstein the chipmunk fell out of the
control booth and tumbled into the pool.

THUNK!

SPLASH!

The giant squid **crashed** into the pool, too. Kenny and I were the last to hit the water . . . and we did the biggest belly flops EVER!

SPLAT!

There was a panicked cry of 'Help!'
Einstein couldn't swim and he was
calling out to Dr Kane in the helicopter.

'You're lucky I'm always here to **lend a
hand,'** Dr Kane called back.

Suddenly, an enormous hand holding
a giant net shot out of the back of the
helicopter and scooped up Einstein.

As the giant squid lay lifeless at the bottom of the pool, Kenny and I breathed a huge sigh of **relief.**

'That was some plan, Ninja Kid,' Kenny said.

'Couldn't have pulled it off without you, H-Dude,' I replied.

We were just about to share a **fist bump** when the giant squid burst back to life!

NINE

'I don't understand,' I said, shocked. 'How can the squid **move** without someone in the control booth?'

'I knew it was REAL!' Kenny replied.

'Suckers!' Dr Kane shouted. 'We can also control the squid with a remote!'

He handed the remote control to Einstein, who directed the squid straight towards us.

'We didn't even get time to celebrate
how **awesome** our dives were!' Kenny
said as we quickly swam away from the
squid.

'Don't worry,' I said. 'I've got **another
plan.**'

'I was afraid you were going to say that!' groaned Kenny. 'Please tell me this one takes place at the **snack bar.** All this squid fighting has given me quite an **appetite!'**

'Sorry, H-Dude, not this time,' I laughed.

'OK!' Kenny said as we climbed out of the pool. 'Talk me through your new plan.'

'While we were diving past the squid,' I said, 'I noticed a **power lever** inside the control booth. I think if we can **turn off**

the power lever, Einstein won't be able to control the squid with the remote.'

'Great idea,' Kenny said. 'Only problem is, neither of us is **small enough** to fit inside the control booth.'

'I know someone that is,' Sarah called out from the stadium.

'Awesome idea, Sarah,' I said.

Kenny and I raced up to them and

the five of us had a lightning-quick

BRAINSTORM.

The giant squid was back to its old, **terrifying** self. Only now, it was being controlled by Einstein from the helicopter.

'We're **so happy** you're back,' Kenny said to the giant squid.

'We've got something to show you,' I added. 'Come with us.'

H-Dude and I swam underneath the arch. Einstein directed the squid's two long tentacles after us.

As the tentacles tried to **snatch us,**
Kenny and I swam round and round the
arch. The tentacles followed us until . . .

they were all tied up in **EPIC**

knots!

'What have you done?' Dr Kane yelled at Einstein. 'My giant squid looks like a giant pretzel! FIX THIS MESS!'

'I can't move them!' Einstein replied, as he manically pressed buttons on the remote control.

'Noodles!' I called out. 'It's your time to shine!'

Noodles barked excitedly then ran down to the pool.

Noodles used one of the entangled tentacles as a ramp to climb up to the control booth and into the giant squid's head!

Once she was inside the control booth, Noodles jumped on the power lever. **It worked!** Noodles had shut down the squid!

She slid back down the tentacle and jumped out of the water. Seconds later, the giant squid sank to the bottom of the pool. **This time it stayed there!**

Dr Kane and Einstein were FURIOUS.

'You're going to pay for this, Ninja Kid and H-Dude!' Dr Kane shouted.

'Yeah, you're going to pay for this, Ninja Kid and H-Dude!' Einstein shouted.

'Don't just repeat what I say!' Dr Kane bellowed at Einstein. 'Come up with **your own** threatening insults!'

I didn't care about Dr Kane and Einstein anymore, I was more worried about the **ULTIMATE NINJA.** Also known as my dad.

'Where's the Ultimate Ninja?' I asked.

'Oh, don't worry about him,' Dr Kane replied. 'He's completing **top-secret** training.'

'Next time you see him,' Einstein said, 'he will be even more **POWERFUL!**'

The evil chipmunk started laughing like a maniac.

'Stop laughing, **you numbskull!**' Dr Kane said. He shot us a dirty look before the helicopter flew off into the distance.

'Thanks for all your help, Sarah and Tiffany,' I said.

'Yeah, no way could we have brought down the giant squid without you,' Kenny said.

'Noodles was the **real hero!**' Sarah said.

'Thanks, Noodles!' Kenny and I said at the same time. Noodles wagged her tail and barked excitedly at us. I'm pretty sure she was the only one that knew we were Nelson and Kenny!

'We've gotta run,' I said.

'Say hi to Nelson and Kenny when you see them,' Kenny added.

'They always **miss out** on the action,' Sarah sighed.

TEN

That night, we told Mum and Grandma about our latest encounter with Dr Kane.

'We would never have been able
to **defeat** the giant squid without
your incredible underwater breathing
necklaces,' I said.

'And thanks to your animal translation
helmets,' Kenny said, 'I got to chat to a
turtle, a seal and a dolphin.'

'Don't forget a Moodle!' I said.

'I hope the training Dr Kane's making the Ultimate Ninja do isn't too gruelling,' I said.

'Dr Kane **needs your dad** more than your dad needs Dr Kane,' Grandma said. 'He won't hurt him.'

'I'm sorry you didn't get to see him today,' Mum said sadly.

'You're going to see him again one day, Mum,' I said. 'And he won't be the Ultimate Ninja. He'll just be **Dad.**'

'I hope you're right,' Mum said.

'I know I am,' I replied.

I gave Mum a hug.

Then Grandma, Kenny and Noodles joined the hug. It was like being **squashed** by the giant squid all over again!

Except that it felt like **home.**

READ THEM ALL!

NINJA KID 10 COMING SOON!